# Caribbean animals

by Dawne Allette
illustrated by Alan Baker

To Lourdes with love, from Grandma
D.A.

With love to Charlotte
A.B.

Thanks to Christian




CARIBBEAN ANIMALS
TAMARIND BOOKS 9781870516679

Published in Great Britain by Tamarind Books,
a division of Random House Children's Books
A Random House Group Company

This edition published 2004
Reprinted 2008

3 5 7 9 10 8 6 4 2





TAMARIND BOOKS
61–63 Uxbridge Road, London, W5 5SA

www.**tamarindbooks**.co.uk
www.**kidsatrandomhouse**.co.uk

Addresses for companies within The Random House Group Limited can be found at:
www.randomhouse.co.uk/offices.htm

THE RANDOM HOUSE GROUP Limited Reg. No. 954009

A CIP catalogue record for this book is available from the British Library.

Printed and bound in Singapore

# Welcome to the Caribbean

My name is Ned.

I'll show you the animals from A to Z.

An agouti is making faces at me.

A butterfly chases a bumble bee.

A crocodile has its mouth open wide.

A donkey is taking a boy for a ride.

Look! A mouse is building a house.

What else can I see
From up here in my tree?

Egrets

all dressed in white.

Flamboyant flamingoes
ready for flight.

A grasshopper is looking for a tasty treat.

Hummingbird is having something sweet to eat.

There's that mouse building his house.

Iguana
makes music on
a steel band pan.

A jellyfish
floats like a colourful fan.

A kiskadee is trying to reach the sky.

A ladybird slips away with a sigh.

And the mouse is building his house.

What's to my left?
What's to my right?

A manicou here,

a mongoose there,

a frisky nanny goat, without a care.

A baby octopus wallows in a pool.

Parrots are learning to talk
at school.
That mouse has a roof on his house!

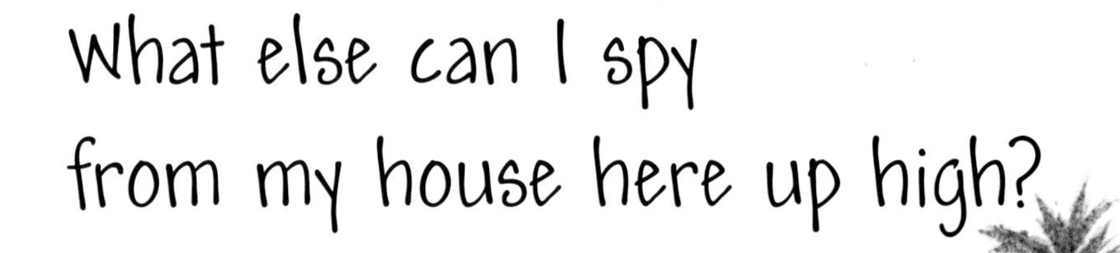

What else can I spy
from my house here up high?

A quail

is making her summer nest.

Brer rabbit is hopping home for a rest.

A spider slickly
weaves his house.

A tortoise turns to look at the mouse.

Urchins galore cling to the shore.

One viper, two vipers, three vipers, four...

A **whale** is splashing far away in the ocean.

The x-ray fish

are disturbed by the motion.

A yellow finch flies up higher than high.

Is that zandoli trying to fly?

That's all I can see,
now it's time for bed.
Goodbye to the creatures
from A to Z.

That mouse has moved into his house.

# Caribbean animals

The Caribbean is the land around the Caribbean Sea, including Central America, the Caribbean islands (from Cuba to Trinidad and Tobago) and the north coast of South America. The animals shown here all come from different parts of the Caribbean to give a flavour of the rich variety of animal life in the hot, tropical climate.

**Agouti** – a small rodent that lives near water. It can jump 2m up into the air and barks in alarm when threatened. It eats fruit, vegetables and leaves.
**Butterfly (Scarce bamboo page)** – flies high up in the forest. Lantana (the red flower in the picture) is its favourite nectar source. Males and females look alike.
**Bumble bee** – same as the European bee. It has quite a short tongue, so it prefers to feed on plants with daisy-type flowers. If a flower is too deep and it cannot reach the nectar, the bee bites a hole near the base of the petals. Then it pushes its tongue through to drink the nectar.
**Crocodile (Spectacled caiman)** – a small crocodile that lives in swamps and rivers but prefers still waters. If the water gets too salty it goes to sleep. The bony ridge between its eyes gives it its name.
**Donkey** – has been bred by human beings for 6,000 years. It can carry heavy loads for long periods with little food and water. It eats hay, grass and any kind of vegetable.
**Egret (Great white)** – a large white bird that stands at the water's edge in huge flocks to feed. It snatches its prey (fish and frogs) from the water with a quick snap of its long, bendy neck.
**Flamingo (Pink)** – a large bird that gets its colouring from the shellfish and algae it feeds on. It feels most comfortable standing on one leg.
**Grasshopper (Abracris flavolineata)** – a jumping insect with stiff wings. It has a large compound eye, made up of thousands of single lenses, on each side of its head. It has six legs. Its hind legs are long and strong, with big thigh muscles to help it jump.
**Hummingbird (Ribbon tailed)** – a tiny bird that flutters its wings very fast so that it can hover beside flowers. It feeds on nectar, which it sucks up through its long beak. This one is the Jamaican national bird.
**Iguana (Green)** – a large lizard that lives in trees. It has a crest of spines along its neck which gives it the look of a prehistoric monster. It can grow up to 1.8m in length, about half of this being a strong whip-like tail. It is an excellent swimmer.
**Jellyfish (Compass)** – moves through the water by pulsating movements of its bell. It grows up to 30cm across. It is omnivorous (eats lots of different food), feeding especially on zooplankton (microscopic sea creatures). It catches prey in its tentacles and carries it to the four long arms around its central mouth.
**Kiskadee** – a bold, noisy bird that makes a distinctive sound (kis-ka-dee – which in French sounds like "qu'est-ce qu'il a dit", meaning "what is he saying?"). It perches over water and plunges down to catch fish, frogs and tadpoles. After a while it has to dry out and switches to catching flying insects. It also eats lizards and baby birds, and seeds in winter.
**Ladybird (Blood-red)** – this ladybird often has no spots at all. Ladybirds feed on the larvae (young) of other insects and are loved by farmers because they eat the pests that feed on their crops.

**Mongoose** – not a native of the Caribbean, it was introduced from India to catch rats in the sugar cane plantations. Now it has become a pest itself, as it eats birds and other wildlife, as well as carrying diseases. It lives on land but can swim.

**Manicou** – or opossum, a marsupial mammal, which carries its babies in a pouch like kangaroos and koalas. It is 60–90cm long and weighs 2–5kg. Its hind feet have a toe that looks like a thumb, a bit like we have on our hands. This toe helps the manicou climb well. Its naked, scaly tail can wrap around branches. The manicou can even hang from its tail for short periods. It is a gentle animal, but it will hiss and growl and show its sharp teeth when frightened. If attacked it lies still and pretends to be dead. It also gives off a foul smelling substance.

**Goat (Saanen)** – brought over from Europe, this is a hardy white goat with horns. The nanny (female) goat, as well as the billy (male), has a long beard.

**Octopus (Caribbean reef)** – a small, nocturnal species. It has special cells in its skin, called chromatophores, which allow it to change colour instantly. Its beak, located at the base of its arms, is used to bite and sometimes inject a poison which can paralyse prey.

**Parrot (St Vincent amazon)** – lives in humid forests at the foot of mountains. It can be seen singly, in pairs and in flocks of up to thirty birds, high up in the trees where it is well camouflaged. It is very noisy and makes a loud quaw... quaw sound when it flies. It is endangered because of habitat destruction, hunting and illegal trade.

**Quail (Bobwhite)** – brought to the Caribbean from the United States. It lives on the ground in brushy fields. It eats seeds, fruit, plant parts, spiders, and insects.

**Rabbit (Eastern cottontail)** – not native, but brought from the United States for breeding and now wild.

**Spider (Golden silk)** – makes large, sticky, golden webs. It is not dangerous and will bite only if held or pinched. The bite can be a little painful and produces a red mark, which soon fades. It eats a wide variety of small to medium-sized flying insects, including flies, bees, wasps, and small moths and butterflies, as well as small beetles and dragonflies.

**Tortoise (Red footed)** – lives in woods and eats fruit that has fallen onto the ground, leaves and even flowers. It drinks a lot of water. It doesn't hibernate in the warm climate The biggest tortoise of this kind on record was 44.38cm long!

**Urchin (Variegated sea)** – about 76mm across, it lives on the bottom of the sea, where there is sand or gravel and a lot of plant life as well as among mangroves. It is usually camouflaged, with bits of shell, plant material, and other debris caught in its spines.

**Urchin (Atlantic purple sea)** – about 50mm across, it lives on rock and shells, among seaweed, in tidepools. It is omnivorous (eats anything) and will eat algae, sponges, coral polyps, mussels, dead or dying urchins and other animals.

**Viper (Fer de lance)** – a deadly pit viper, named by French settlers because of its lance-shaped head. It can grow to a length of 2.5m, but usually only reaches about 1.5m long. It has long, hollow, poison-filled fangs that inject venom from special glands into the victim's body. It feeds on insects and lizards when young, but an adult will kill opossums, frogs, lizards, small snakes, birds and rodents.

**Whale (Fin)** – large, slender whale similar to the blue whale. An old individual can reach a length of 25m or more, with females on average slightly larger than the males. It migrates to colder feeding grounds near either the North or South Poles during spring and summer. It returns to warmer tropical waters during autumn and winter to mate and calve (have babies). It feeds mainly on krill but also eats schooling fish, such as herring, cod, mackerel and sardine.

**X-ray fish** – live in groups in calm, coastal waters and thick swamps. They feed on worms, small crustaceans and insects. They have a peaceful character and delicate colours. They are very small.

**Yellow finch** – a small, brightly coloured bird that nests in grasslands and open fields near the coast.

**Zandoli** – a small anole lizard which lives in grass and stumpy brush. It can change colour, just like a chameleon (to which it is not related).